WAR DOG

Chris Ryan

EDGE
FRANKLIN WATTS

LONDON·SYDNEY

First published in 2013
by Franklin Watts

Text © Chris Ryan 2013
Cover design by Peter Scoulding

Franklin Watts
338 Euston Road
London NW1 3BH

Franklin Watts Australia
Level 17/207 Kent Street
Sydney, NSW 2000

A CIP catalogue record for this book
is available from the British Library.

Slava Gerj/Shutterstock: front cover c.
Anna Kucherova/Shutterstock: front cover b.
lolloj/Shutterstock: front cover top.

(ebook) ISBN: 978 1 4451 2346 2
(pb) ISBN: 978 1 4451 2345 5
(Library ebook) ISBN: 978 1 4451 2579 4

1 3 5 7 9 10 8 6 4 2

Printed in Great Britain

Franklin Watts is a division of
Hachette Children's Books,
an Hachette UK company.
www.hachette.co.uk

Contents

Chapter One:

THE GREEN ZONE

You think it's funny, do you? You think it's a laugh to stare at me limping through the park? How old are you? Not much younger than I was when I lost my leg.

Yeah, that's right. Eighteen years old. My whole life ahead of me. Still think I look funny, hey? Go on, have a good giggle at the man with the plastic foot.

What? You want to know how it happened?

Don't mess me around. Seriously, are you sure?

Alright then. Let's sit down on this park bench here. I'm sorry, I'm a little out of breath. It's tiring going around on these crutches. I was very fit back in my army days. But ... well, those days are gone. My name's Jamie, by the way. Pleased to meet you.

***

It happened on a hot afternoon. Correction: it happened on a *scorching* hot afternoon. Every summer's day in Afghanistan is a scorcher. You sometimes think you'll never be cool again.

We'd been on patrol since before dawn. Our route had taken us into the Green Zone.

What's the Green Zone?

Well, in the south of Afghanistan,
most of the terrain is desert.
Dry. Barren. But there are rivers
that carry water down from the
nearby mountains. The banks of
these rivers are fertile — good
for growing stuff. That's why
they call it the Green Zone, and
it's where they grow fruit and
vegetables. Most of the locals live
in the Green Zone. Most of the
enemy, too. They're called the

Taliban — you've probably heard
of them on the news. All they
want to do is kill British soldiers.
And if they can't kill them, they'll
make do with maiming them.
Loads of my friends out there
have lost arms. Or legs. Or both.

Friends. That's what being in
the army is all about. You make
friends. You look after your
friends. You watch each other's
back. But there was this one guy
in my platoon who wasn't really
a friend. The opposite, in fact. I
used to laugh at him. We all did.

A bit like you were laughing at me just then. His name was Sam. Sam Maguire. And why did we laugh at him? Because he was different, I suppose.

You see, Sam's best friend wasn't another soldier. His best friend was a sniffer dog called Charlie.

Chapter Two:
WAR DOG

Didn't you know they had dogs
in the army? You'd be surprised.
Attack dogs. Patrol dogs. Sentry
dogs. Search and rescue dogs. But
Charlie? He was one of the best.

You wouldn't think it to look at him. A raggedy-looking thing. A springer spaniel with puppy-dog eyes. His ears touched the ground when he drank from his bowl. But that dog could sniff out a bomb from a hundred metres. It was Sam who taught him to do it. Together, they uncovered more bombs than any other team in the British Army.

And the Taliban, they like their bombs. We called them IEDs out there — Improvised Explosive Devices. They're almost impossible to see. If you tread on one, you're coming home in a box. At least, the bits of you that they can find are. But Charlie could sniff them out, and Sam could defuse them. I don't know how many lives they must've saved. Hundreds, probably.

They were a strange couple, though. Inseparable. Back at base, Sam would never hang out with the rest of us. He just wanted to be with his dog. We'd all be playing *Call of Duty* together while Sam would be

grooming Charlie. Brushing
the desert sand out of his fur.
Checking his paws. Keeping him
company. Of course, we used
to tease him. You know the sort
of thing. "Hey, Sam, what is it
with you and Charlie. Does he
remind you of your girlfriend or
something?" But I never saw Sam
get cross. He just smiled and
shrugged it off. Then he went
back to brushing Charlie's coat.
He loved that dog. And the dog
loved him back. Charlie would do
anything for Sam.

He would even follow him into
the Green Zone.

Chapter Three:
UNDER FIRE

It was three o'clock in the afternoon. We'd been sheltering from the midday sun in an abandoned courtyard on the edge of a village. We were just getting ready to leave, hoisting our rucksacks onto our backs, when we heard gunfire.

You never get used to it. The crack of an AK47. The whoosh of a rocket-propelled grenade as it hurtles over your head. It stops your heart for a few seconds.

"RPG!" someone shouted at the top of their voice. We all hit the ground. I heard the rocket explode just beyond the courtyard. Then I heard a shower of shrapnel hitting the ground.

I looked round to check none of my friends had been hit. All the guys — there were sixteen of us — were lying on their fronts. So was Charlie. Unlike the men, he didn't look scared. He was alongside Sam, still, but alert.

There was a moment of silence. And then the enemy opened fire again. We could tell they were close. Between thirty and fifty metres. I tried to work out how many guns were firing. I couldn't. There were too many. This was a heavy attack.

Our patrol commander got on the radio back to base. "Zero, this is patrol Delta Tango Five. We have heavy small arms fire from the north. Request pick-up, repeat, request pick-up."

The gunfire fell quiet. That made me feel more nervous. It meant the enemy were on the move.

The patrol commander got to his feet and jabbed one finger in a westerly direction. Made sense. The enemy fire had come from the north. South or east would have taken us back into the heart of the Green Zone. West was our only option. We left that dusty courtyard through a door in the western wall, treading quietly and in single file.

My L85 assault rifle was cocked and locked. I held it across my chest with the barrel pointing downwards, and followed the guy in front. His name was Doug Talbot. He was a thin, lanky Scottish lad, and a good friend. I kept five metres from him. When you're marching in single file, you mustn't bunch up. If you're too close together, you make an easy target.

Our path took us away from the village, along a shallow ditch towards a field of corn. It was the size of a football pitch. The corn was as tall as me, but it only came up to Doug Talbot's shoulders. Tall bloke, was Doug.

Once we'd reached the cover of the cornfield, the patrol commander gave us the lowdown. "OK, lads," he said, sweat clearing lines through the dirt on his face. "On the other side of this field, there's fifty metres of open ground. Beyond that, there's an abandoned compound. We can take cover there until a chopper arrives to pick us up."

"But, Sarge," someone said, "if we walk across open ground we'll be a target..."

The patrol commander nodded grimly. "Check for snipers before you step out of the cornfield. And don't walk: run."

Doug led the way across the cornfield, keeping his shoulders hunched and his head down. I went next. Behind me was Sam, and behind him, Charlie. The rest of the platoon followed.

It took about three minutes to cross the cornfield. At the far side, just like the commander had said, there was a stretch of open ground. Fifty metres away was the abandoned compound.

Doug was nervously licking his

lips when I caught up with him. Together we peered out from the edge of the cornfield. We were looking for snipers, but couldn't see anyone. Just the compound. It shimmered in the heat haze.

Doug looked at me.

I looked back at him.

"I'll go first," he said.

We clenched our fists and touched our knuckles together. That was something we always did.

"Take care, buddy," I said.

He nodded.

And then he walked to his death.

Chapter Four:
THE BLAST

Looking back, I know what our
mistake was. We didn't have
enough respect for our enemy.
They'd forced us to take this
escape route. We never worked

out that they had us exactly where they wanted us. In the middle of a minefield.

Doug moved quickly. He was about ten metres out into open ground when I followed. I had to stop myself from sprinting. If I caught up with him, we'd be bunched up. And I've already told you what that means. So I ran ten metres behind — just looking straight ahead. Doug was halfway across the open ground. The compound looked so close...

And then Doug stepped directly onto an IED pressure plate.

It's the noise that gets you at first. Forget all those explosions you've seen in the movies. This was like being in the middle of a thunderclap. Then the shock waves hit you.

Have you ever been punched? This is a hundred times worse.

I was thrown back several metres, and landed on my back. I couldn't see anything through the cloud

of dust. I shouted Doug's name.
No reply. I heard something thud
onto the ground right next to me.
It was an arm, severed just below
the shoulder. I knew then that
Doug was dead.

I'm sorry. I know my voice is
breaking up. It's a hard thing to
talk about. I'll be alright in a
second.

Rubble was falling on me. A
shower of stones. But then
something hit my own leg that
wasn't a stone. It slammed into

my shin. I couldn't see what it was because of the dust. And at first my leg didn't hurt. But then the dust settled. I saw a twisted hunk of metal sticking out of my lower leg. My trousers were ripped. And there was blood.

A lot of blood.

The pain hit me suddenly. It's hard to describe how bad it was. To start with, it felt as if all the blood in my leg had turned to ice. I tried to sit up and pull the shrapnel out. A terrible twist of agony shrieked up through my knee. I fell back to the ground again. I think I was screaming. Yelling to my mates to come and help me. But as I looked back towards the cornfield, I could see that the patrol commander had ordered them not to step out into the open ground. No one was coming to help. I didn't blame them. Where you find one IED, you normally find loads. A single step could kill any one of them. They were afraid. Who wouldn't be?

There was one exception.
Charlie, the sniffer dog, was
already poking his nose through
the edge of the cornfield. And
Sam, his handler, was by his side.
He had one hand on the dog's
head. His eyes were narrowed in
concentration.

The man and his dog stepped out
into open ground.

Chapter Five:
THE SNIPER

Charlie and Sam had to cover about twenty metres. Doesn't sound like a lot, does it? Well, believe me — if a single step could kill you, it might as well be twenty miles.

The dog went first. His nose was close to the ground. He inched forwards, sniffing the desert floor. And even though I was screaming — oh, boy, the pain — he didn't look up once. Sam walked directly behind him. He had a plastic bottle full of white chalk dust. He used this to mark a safe passage behind him.

My world started to spin. I no longer had the energy to scream. But I still had the energy to be scared. And I was scared when I saw the dog stop.

He was only ten metres away from me. He barked once, then sat down.

His handler crouched on all fours. He stretched out one hand and gently scraped the dusty earth in front of the dog. I couldn't see what he found, but it must have been a pressure plate. Sam made a chalk circle around it. The dog turned ninety degrees and boxed round the IED. Its nose was back down to the ground.

I think I must have passed out

then. The next thing I knew, Charlie was licking my face. I heard Sam's voice. "Stay with us, buddy," he said. "We're going to get you out of here." I felt a needle puncture my trousers and slip into my good leg. Sam was giving me morphine. Seconds later, the drug hit my bloodstream.

It's a weird feeling, morphine. It doesn't take the pain away. It just stops you caring about it. I felt drowsy as Sam lifted me up in his arms and followed Charlie,

step by slow step, towards the
compound. How long did it take?
I couldn't tell you. All I know is
that without the dog, we'd never
have made it there in safety.

Have you ever heard the sound of
a Chinook helicopter? They're the
ones with two sets of rotors.

When you're out on the ground,
it's the best sound you can hear.
I couldn't see well, but I knew a
Chinook was coming in to land.
I heard voices. Army medics had
surrounded me. Two of them

carried a stretcher. Sam laid me on it. "You're going to be okay, mate," he said. "The medics will take care of you. Me and Charlie need to get back and help the others." His hands and clothes were covered in my blood. The sun was shining behind his head. The dog was sitting patiently by his side.

If the sound of a Chinook is the best you'll ever hear, the sound of an enemy sniper is the worst. A shot rang out. I saw a flash of red as it hit Sam just above his ear.

He fell to the ground.

Actually, I was wrong. That wasn't
the worst sound I've ever heard.
The worst sound was when Charlie
began to howl as his master fell
dead to the ground.

I'll never forget that howl.
Sometimes it wakes me up when
I'm sleeping.

Chapter Six: GOODBYE

I remember nothing more of that day, or of the day that followed. I woke up in the camp hospital. The doctors told me they'd had to remove my leg just above the knee. I'll tell you a strange thing. Even though I'd lost the leg, I could still feel it. It still hurt. Sometimes it still does. Like a memory of pain.

I didn't feel sorry for myself. How could I, when two men had died? The nurses wanted me to stay in bed, but I made them lift me into a wheelchair. Doug's and Sam's coffins were being sent home that day. I needed to say goodbye to my mates.

They wheeled me out onto the

airfield. Two hundred men were standing silently in a line. They all stood still, wearing full uniform in the fierce heat. Beyond them stood a Hercules aircraft. Its loading ramp was open. The two coffins stood on wooden supports between the men and the plane. Each was covered with a Union Jack. The chaplain read from a prayer book. Sweat poured down his face.

And in front of one coffin was Charlie. He was lying down. His head was pressed against the sandy desert floor. His eyes looked up at his master's coffin. In the two days since the blast, he had grown thinner. His fur was matted. He didn't move.

I hardly heard what the chaplain said. I was too busy looking at the coffins. At Charlie. When fourteen men stepped forward to carry the coffins onto the Hercules, the dog stood up. He followed the coffins up the loading ramp. Men, coffins and dog disappeared into the hot belly of the aircraft.

Three minutes later the men reappeared. They were no longer carrying the coffins, but one of them held Charlie by his collar. He had to drag the dog. Charlie whimpered in protest. He kept his feet rigid. In the end, it took two men to remove him from the aircraft.

You've never seen anything worse than the way that poor dog howled as the ramp closed. Nobody could stop him chasing the Hercules down the runway. In the air, the plane dipped a wing as a gesture of respect. Charlie howled and howled. Then the plane disappeared into the Afghan sky, and he was silent again.

I wanted to take Charlie back into the camp hospital. To look after him. But they wouldn't let me. I still saw him, though. Each day, someone would push me round the camp in a wheelchair. And each day, Charlie would be sitting in the same place. Outside his master's sleeping quarters. As if he was waiting for Sam to come home.

The dog didn't eat. I watched him get thinner by the day. He met my eyes every time I passed. There was something human in his stare. It felt like there was a bond between us. And I suppose there was. We'd both watched Sam die, after all.

On the fifth day after Sam's coffin was sent back, Charlie wasn't in his usual place. I had a bad feeling about it. I asked the nurse who was pushing my wheelchair if we could look for him. It didn't take long to find him.

In the middle of the camp there
is a small war memorial. The
names of all the British soldiers
who have died in Afghanistan
are engraved there. Charlie was
curled on the ground in front of
it. His big eyes didn't look up as I
passed. His chest didn't rise and
fall. He looked like he was asleep.
But it was the kind of sleep you
never wake up from.

We buried Charlie where he lay.
It seemed like the right thing to
do. I couldn't help, of course.
But I watched as my friends dug

the hole and lowered him into the earth. It felt as if Sam was with us in spirit. Saying goodbye to his friend. Or, maybe, saying hello again. Welcoming him to wherever it is we go when we die. At least, that's what I like to think.

***

Anyway, I've kept you too long. Your folks will be wondering where you are. You'd better go, but thanks for listening, you know. Don't worry about me.

I'll be fine. You get used to a false
leg after a while. And whatever
you do, don't feel sorry for me.
Because remember: thanks to
a brave dog and his handler, I
escaped with my life.

That makes me one of the lucky
ones.

ANDREW FUSEK PETERS

Breathe
AND YOU DIE

From the author of Ravenwood

RIVETS

EDGE

If you enjoyed reading *War Dog*, you might also like *Breathe And You Die* by Andrew Fusek Peters.

Matt wakes up in a room he doesn't recognise.
The room is full of smoke.
The smoke is toxic. If he breathes it in, he'll die.

Matt and his friend Leah are caught up
in a madman's plan for revenge on their school.
But before Matt can save his friends,
he must save himself...

Buy online at
www.franklinwatts.co.uk.
978 1 4451 2313 4 paperback
978 1 4451 2316 5 eBook

Turn over to read an extract from
Breathe And You Die.

7 p.m.

Matt woke up coughing. The smell in his nose was rank, a mix of rotten eggs and dead meat. *Where was he? And why did his head hurt?* He slowly opened his eyes. *Weird.* He was lying on bare floorboards in a room he'd never seen in his life. He still wore his school clothes, now scuffed and torn. If this was a dream, it was convincing. Thick smoke hovered a few inches above his head. More of it poured in from a vent high in the ceiling. Here, down by the floor, the air was almost clear.

It didn't take a science degree to know the smoke was poison. If he sat up, and breathed it in, he'd be dead. Matt tried to think. Last thing he remembered, he was leaving school late after his karate lesson. His Kata had been good and the Sensei, his teacher, was pleased with Matt's progress. *What else?* There'd been a van with tinted windows, slowing down alongside him. Then ...

nothing. He coughed again, he could feel the gas exploring his lungs, trying to shut him down for good.

It didn't make sense. He was an ordinary year 9 boy, who went to a boring school. A brown belt in Shotokan Karate, even with a second stripe, was hardly a threat. Every second he lay there thinking, the smoke above his head grew thicker. He had to get out. Apart from the bump on his head, he appeared to be in one piece. Matt crawled as close to the floor as possible towards the door. The room narrowed into a corridor. When he finally got to the end and reached up with his arm, the door was firmly locked and the letter box was nailed down. *Who would do this to him? It was mad!* He slid backwards. Maybe he'd have better luck with the window.

He grabbed a deep lungful of clean air and stood up, using both arms to try and slide the window

open. The smoke made his eyes
smart. Why wouldn't it budge?
He looked again. Window lock.
Damn! Think Matty. Think! Of
course — the dirty plastic chair
by the window. It had metal legs.
He knelt down to take another
breath and grabbed the chair,
swinging with all his might against
the glass.

Also in the **RIVETS** series

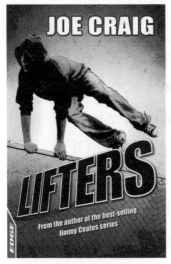

978 1 4451 0555 0 pb
978 1 4451 0850 6 eBook

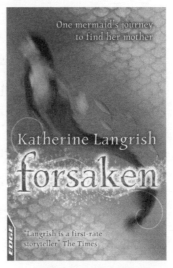

978 1 4451 0557 4 pb
978 1 4451 1073 8 eBook

978 1 4451 0556 7 pb
978 1 4451 0849 0 eBook

978 1 4451 0707 3 pb
978 1 4451 1072 1 eBook

Also available from **EDGE**.
CRIME TEAM adventures by The 2Steves,
where YOU crack the case!

978 0 7496 9283 4 pb
978 1 4451 0843 8 eBook

978 0 7496 9284 1 pb
978 1 4451 0844 5 eBook

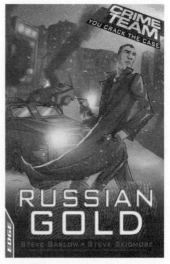

978 0 7496 9286 5 pb
978 1 4451 0845 2 eBook

978 0 7496 9285 8 pb
978 1 4451 0846 9 eBook